MARVEL

AN ORIGINAL GRAPHIC NOVEL

SHANG-CHI

AND THE QUEST FOR IMMORTALITY

BY
VICTORIA YING

COLORS BY
IAN HERRING

LETTERS BY
VC'S TRAVIS LANHAM

graphix

AN IMPRINT OF
■SCHOLASTIC

LAUREN BISOM, Senior Editor
CAITLIN O'CONNELL, Associate Editor
ANTHONY GAMBINO, Publication Design
JENNIFER GRÜNWALD, Senior Editor, Special Projects
SVEN LARSEN, VP Licensed Publishing
JEFF YOUNGQUIST, VP Production & Special Projects
DAVID GABRIEL, SVP Print, Sales & Marketing
C.B. CEBULSKI, Editor in Chief

MICHAEL PETRANEK, Editorial Director, AFK & Graphix Media, Scholastic
SALENA MAHINA, Designer, Scholastic
YAFFA JASKOLL, Creative Director, Scholastic

ISBN 978-1-338-83372-0

10 9 8 7 6 5 4 3 2   23 24 25 26 27

Printed in the U.S.A.   40

First edition, October 2023

Art by Victoria Ying and Ian Herring
Letters by VC's Travis Lanham

**For every
son and daughter
finding their way.**

—VY

CHAPTER ONE

...And then the monkey king, Sun Wukong, began his battle with Nezha...

And then does he fight the dragon prince?

No, Shi-Hua, that's another story altogether!

What does it matter? All these fairy tales are made up.

I'll have you know that people once said that your father's power was a fairy tale.

Lots of fairy tales are based on facts. Some people think that the power of the Five Weapons Society is nothing more than a legend.

But that's just wrong.

Fairy tales and legends are often a starting point for power, Shang-Chi. Your father has the world's greatest collection of legends in his archive.

So, you're saying that...for example... maybe the lady on the moon really did float up there because of immortal candy?

Yes.

And maybe the god Nezha really did come out of a ball of flesh cleaved by his father?

Why not?

And maybe the immortal peach grove from *Journey to the West* is *real*?!

Seems as plausible as anything else.

Immortal peaches?

Yes, Shi-Hua...

FWSSSH

Why can't we go see the scrolls of legend, Brother?

÷Sigh÷ Shi-Hua, because it is forbidden.

But *why* is it forbidden?

I don't know! Because Father says it is. Now be quiet, I'm trying to listen.

CLICK... CLICK... TAK TAK... WHIRRRR...

CREEEAKK

Now, time for bed.

Prepare the carriage. I will leave first thing in the morning.

But, sire, why the hurry? The boy is just beginning to grow into his power.

I'm aware of that, but it seems you and all the other houses could do with a reminder of my strength. I must secure my magic in any way necessary.

I would never question your power, sire.

Perfection, Priestess, that is all I demand of you, of my men, and of the boy.

Anything less is failure.

Sometimes, you're really annoying, but thanks.

Of course. We're in this together. Always.

How long will you be going for?

As long as necessary. Remember, Son, keep practicing. You have the power, make sure to use it wisely. Do not disappoint me.

I—

Yes, Father.

24

Not another late-night visit to the archives?

Tien-a, Shi-Hua. You have to stop doing that.

Tell me what you're doing.

I'm doing my duty. I'm helping Father.

You're going to try to find the peach orchard, aren't you?

There's no sense in bringing it up to Father if it's not real. I just want to see it for myself first— If I bring back a peach—

Then he'll finally be happy with you.

Together?

Not this time.

I can make sure nobody notices you're gone...for a while anyway. I can buy you some time to find the orchard and come back.

Really?

You just have to promise to come back.

Thanks.

Get going, I can smell the bao buns, which means Fu-Chang is coming.

Ack!

You'll have to be quieter than that to defeat the stone guardian!

I've never been past here before.

CHAPTER
TWO

Ma'am! I'm looking for— Well, I'm not exactly sure how to say this.

Huh?

I'M LOOKING FOR—

Hah??

VWOOM

Hello, Mrs. Wong!

What in the world is this?

Why is everyone dressed so strangely?

Hey!

Look where you're going! weirdo.

VOO OOM

Listen, I think we got off on the wrong foot. My name is Lu. I promise, no more tricks.

My father always said to watch out for villains.

You really do talk like you're in a Chinese drama.

Let me make it up to you.

First, let's get you some clothes so you can fit in better. You stick out like a poppy among daisies.

Thanks.

Hey, you kids!

RUN!

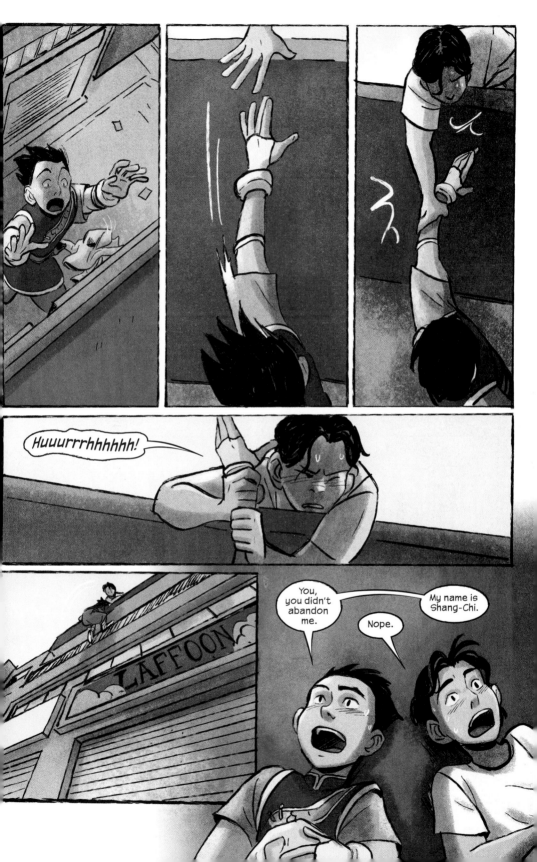

A very important mission. I see!

I need to find something... something for my father.

I wouldn't know what that's like. I don't have parents.

Oh... Hey, no big deal. I'm just one of dozens of kids here without them.

We all rely on one another here.

We need to trust each other.

Trust...

Okay.

You're right, time for a break. Let's feast!

Have you heard the story of the monkey king and the immortal peaches?

Mmffmff.

I'm looking for the peach grove. I think it's real. I need it for my father.

Wow, this thing looks...

I was gonna say expensive.

Real.

I have an idea. I know who we can talk to. Auntie Fan knows everything about old mythology.

Really?

Yeah, and she's not far from here.

Lu—

Tien-a! You scared me!

That boy, the one you are speaking to.

He's the son of Zheng Zu.

Do one worthwhile thing in your lousy life. Don't make me regret saving you from the river.

Bring him to me.

Once I have the boy... I will finally have my revenge.

There you are!

Had to take a leak.

Gross.

But good news! We're here.

Fan's Tea

Wow.

Welcome, welcome!

Well— Oh.

Hi, Auntie Fan! I brought a friend. This is Shang-Chi.

Lu... come here for another free meal?

Not at all! Shang-Chi needs help.

Oh? And what can I help you with?

Um... well...

I'm on a quest.

A quest, you say? That sounds serious indeed.

It is.

I'm searching for the peaches of immortality.

This scroll...

You were right to come to me. As it so happens—

KNOCK KNOCK KNOCK

Yes?

Hello, Mrs. Fan. We are looking for a pair of thieves.

Thieves, you say? How terrible.

They've stolen clothes off the line, and many vendors have said that they've had food taken.

Mumble mumble mumble...

CHAPTER
THREE

Everyone, this is Shang-Chi.

What are you doing, Lu? You know Uncle Rat doesn't like strangers in our camp.

He wanted this one.

Shang-Chi...

A-Again?

You don't remember?

Ah, but you were so small. I suppose all is forgiven. I am known as Uncle Rat. And my dear Lu has brought you to me.

Please, don't hurt him.

Are you commanding me?

...

Lu? I thought— Did you bring me here to get eaten?

HAHAHA! You would think that you of all people would know something about filial piety... I'm the closest thing Lu has to a father. Even a street rat can learn respect.

"You do not remember, but when you were just a baby of one year... Your father tested you.

"To be a worthy son, you had to face challenges on your first birthday.

"Would you cry out? Or would you be brave?

"You were not frightened. Small as you were, you held your ground.

"You were a true son of Zheng Zu.

"Like me.

"Of course, I was jealous.

"So I volunteered for an experimental procedure. I would undergo a process that would bind my DNA with an animal and make me stronger, stronger than you could ever be.

"But something went wrong.

"I was ruined now.

"I gave him everything. And he abandoned me.

"All I wanted was his approval. And I got this.

"And that was far from the end of it. He kept having children. More heirs for his army.

"Only one other passed the trial. The rest...

Argh!

SNAP

Eep!

SQUEEK

I don't know how much longer I can fight...

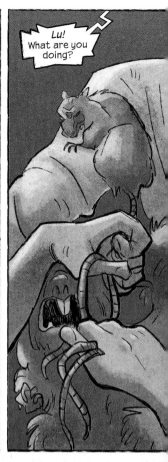

Sorry, little dude.

Won't they be after us?

Nah, that was one of my secret passages. Uncle Rat doesn't know about it.

Why did you help me?

I guess I thought I needed Uncle Rat's approval, but if that's what it takes to get it... it just didn't seem worth it.

I'm sorry. I had no idea about any of this.

Well. I better start planning my escape. There's no way that Uncle Rat will let me back in camp after what I did.

Wait.
What if...

...What if we work together? What if we bring the immortal peach back to...our father?

If we brought it back together... maybe you could come back. Live with us at the compound.

I...

I don't even remember Father. This is all I've ever known. But—but I can't go back to the sewers either.

CHAPTER
FOUR

And that's how we escaped from Uncle Rat...

I'm so glad you boys came back. I was worried about you.

I've been waiting for the day that you would leave Uncle Rat's so-called family.

Do you know where we can find the peaches of immortality?

Fan's Tea

71

There are great things in store for you, Shang-Chi, but you cannot achieve them without help.

You want to help me get a peach for my father?

Well, I want to help you, yes. You and Lu. That's all I'll say about it for now.

You boys make quite a pair. You will need each other if you are going to reach the great peach orchard.

So—

You're the goddess who helped Sun Wukong in the legend on his journey to the West!

Yes, I'm glad my reputation precedes me.

And you want to help *us*! Wow!

Here is a map to the peak. The great feast will take place in just a few days' time and all the peaches will be picked...

Not to mention that I can sense Uncle Rat searching for the two of you in the city, so you must leave right away.

That's the end of the line for public transport...

From here on out, we travel like Sun Wukong...

...by foot.

This map hasn't been updated since your old outfit.

At least the mountains have stayed the same.

I'm starving!

We should have packed some of those buns at Auntie Fan's...

The rats probably ate them all by now.

Maybe a nice juicy peach would do the trick.

I'm kidding! I'm kidding!

BONK

Those peaches are powerful... Only Father would be able to handle all that magic in his body.

Father, and his true heir.

78

Wow, I didn't hear it at all. You would think it would be loud, given that size.

Growing up in the gutters... you learn to pay attention.

Come on, we're in this together.

CHAPTER
FIVE

SKREE!

What do we do now?

Huaaahhh!

He's too fast for me to hit!

Oof!

He'll see Lu before he can reach the tree...

But—

Lu! We need to work together.

Just one more thing to do...

That was great thinking back there...

You were so fast...

It's no wonder you're the chosen son.

I couldn't have done it without you.

You probably could have.

Hey...I think...I think it was wrong of Father to discard you... and everyone else.

What do we know? Maybe he saw something inside us that we can't see. He made the right choice with you.

No—

SHRUG

Hehehehe... Thank you, boys, for taking care of the stone guardian.

Uncle Rat!

I've been searching for a way to defeat Zheng Zu, and I had thought that I could take out my revenge on you...but this is a much better idea!

NO!

Now I will be powerful enough to defeat Zheng Zu on my own! I won't need you filthy brats anymore.

HA HA HA HA HA!

I can't hit him!

SNAP

Oof!

The magic of the peach! He's too strong!

Magic...

Urrghhh...

WHA AAMM!

Thieves, it seems.

It looks like we have our perpetrator right here.

Did you boys defeat this monster?

Y-yes, Guan Yin sent us!

Well, looks like we'll need a new guardian for the peach orchard, and this creature, having eaten the peach of strength, will do well...

CLICK

Thank you, boys, for taking care of this! I was supposed to be on duty, so please don't let anyone know!

Oh, we won't!

I think it's best if we leave the peaches. Father can find eternal life on his own...

Yeah.

You know that's not true!

Well, at least I know when I'm going into hostile territory!

Thanks, Shang-Chi. You helped me to see my own value, even if Father doesn't. I have to go back to the camp.

Without Uncle Rat, we're going to have to find our own way to live. I have to help our brothers and sisters.

I'll find you again, someday, when I can leave with Shi-Hua.

We'll be waiting. Me and the other kids.

Yeah...

"...I think I am."

END

VICTORIA YING is a critically acclaimed author and artist living in Los Angeles. She started her career in the arts by falling in love with comic books, which eventually led her to a career working in animation and graphic novels. She loves Japanese curry, putting things in her shopping cart online and taking them out again, and hanging out with her husband and furry friends. Her film credits include *Tangled*, *Wreck-It Ralph*, *Frozen*, *Paperman*, *Big Hero 6*, and *Moana*. She is the illustrator of DC's *Diana: Princess of the Amazons* and the author and illustrator of *City of Secrets* and the sequel *City of Illusion*.

What was that??? I'm coming up!

NO! No, I'm fine, just... tripped.

Embiggen... disembiggen... just...get back to normal!

Finally!

I know, I know.

PRETTY!

Why is your shirt wrinkled? Is that the shirt you slept in???

NO!

...Maybe.

Kamala! Malik, please!

Big rush, can't stop, gotta go to school, bye, Ammi!

Overslept, huh?

Yeah...it's been impossible getting up lately.

Training?

Well, last night it was updating my fic on embiggenfeels.moomblr.com. But training is tiring too!!!

Nakia, A.K.A. *Kiki.*
(But don't call her that.)
Powers: Critical thinking, podcast recommendations

Hey, it's Bruno! Hey, Bruno!

Kamala, you've got a baby hand again.

Kamala, that is some "pull yourself up by your bootstraps" capitalist nonsense.

The Terrigen Mist happened just a few months ago, so you've had your powers for less than a year. Meaning you've been Ms. Marvel less than a *year*. You're doing great, but it's okay to be tired.

I'm not tired. I've just...got a lot on my plate. But it's fine! Looking forward to a day at school.

I mean...you look pretty tired.

I'm not!

Mm...please, Donald Duck... we need your keyblade to beat this Dread Souls boss...

Wake up, Ms. I'm-Not-Tired.

I'm not tired... Just this one class...

This is the last class of the day. You fell asleep in every class.

Last class of the day...

Last class of the day!

Hey, Kamala, you coming to the computer lab today? I've been working on—

Sorry, I've got ten minutes to pick up Malik from daycare and then get to training! Next time!!!

Yeah... Next time...

Thanks, Lauren! Great to see you again, gottagobye!!!

Bye, Kamala...?

Doreen Green, A.K.A. **Squirrel Girl.** Powers: Superhuman speed and agility, cool tail, can talk to squirrels

Miles Morales, A.K.A. **Spider-Man.** Powers: Web-slinging, invisibility, playlist making

Tony Stark, A.K.A. *Iron Man* Powers: Genius inventor, robot suits, being very rich

Tippy Toe, A.K.A. **That Squirrel with the Bow.** Powers: Stealing food from park picnics

As I have a policy of managing only three preteens at a time, maximum, you're all lucky to be here.

So, robots. Don't know what it is about robots, but the bad guys just love making you fight robots. So that's what we're gonna do.

Nice.

Without much ado: the robots.

NICE.

MS. MARVEL, SPIDER-MAN, SQUIRREL GIRL **(A.K.A. TEAM AWESOME NEXT-GEN SUPER HEROES)** VS. RANDO TRAINING BOTS **(A.K.A. TEAM TOTALLY GOING DOWN)**

CRASSHHH!!

Uh-oh. That's not supposed to happen.

THERE'S MORE MARVEL TO EXPLORE!

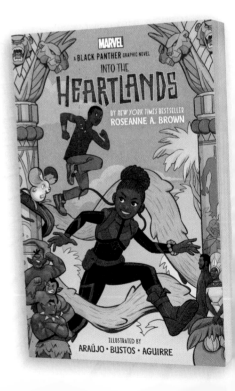

MARVEL

A SPIDER-MAN GRAPHIC NOVEL

MILES MORALES
SHOCK WAVES

WRITTEN BY
JUSTIN A. REYNOLDS

ILLUSTRATED BY
PABLO LEON

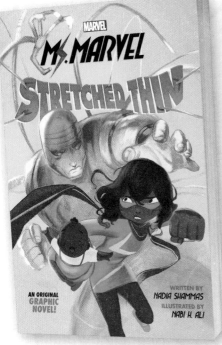

MARVEL

MS. MARVEL
STRETCHED THIN

AN ORIGINAL
GRAPHIC
NOVEL!

WRITTEN BY
NADIA SHAMMAS

ILLUSTRATED BY
NABI H. ALI

MARVEL

AN ORIGINAL GRAPHIC NOVEL BY
#1 NEW YORK TIMES BESTSELLING AUTHOR
ALAN GRATZ
CAPTAIN AMERICA
THE GHOST ARMY

ILLUSTRATED BY
BRENT SCHOONOVER